The Laird's Inheritance

The Laird's Inheritance

George MacDonald

Michael R. Phillips, Editor

BETHANY HOUSE PUBLISHERS
MINNEAPOLIS, MINNESOTA 55438
A Division of Bethany Fellowship, Inc.

Originally published in 1881 as *Warlock o' Glenwarlock* by Sampson Low
Publishing, London, England

Copyright © 1987
Michael R. Phillips
All Rights Reserved

Published by Bethany House Publishers
A Division of Bethany Fellowship, Inc.
6820 Auto Club Road, Minneapolis, Minnesota 55438

Printed in the United States of America

Library of Congress Cataloging-in-Publication Data

MacDonald, George, 1824–1905.
    The laird's inheritance/George MacDonald; Michael R. Phillips, editor.
        p.   cm.
    Rev. ed. of: Warlock o' Glenwarlock.
    This edition has been edited for the modern reader, with much of the Scottish
dialect translated for easier comprehension.
    ISBN 0-87123-903-5 (pbk.)
    I. Phillips, Michael A., 1946–   .   II. MacDonald, George, 1824–
1905. Warlock o' Glenwarlock.   III. Title.
PR4967.W3   1987   823'.8—dc19   87-18434

Table of Contents

Introduction

George MacDonald (1824–1905)—Scottish novelist, poet, preacher, essayist, and literary figure of the late 19th century—was a household name in Britain and many parts of the United States between 1870 and 1910. His more than fifty books sold in the multiple millions, and he was widely recognized in the first rank among an impressive roster of English-speaking authors.

However, in the seventy years following his death, MacDonald's fame, like that of many of his Victorian colleagues, diminished; one by one his books went out of print. By the latter half of the 20th century his name as a literary force had vanished from sight, with the exception here and there of pockets of interest in his fantasy and fairy stories. But in the genre for which he was most widely known in his own time—the adult Victorian novel, of which he wrote approximately thirty—not a single book remained in print.

One of his own books, however, proved prophetic concerning the spiritual truths which MacDonald planted in his lifetime but which seemingly had been forgotten. In *Paul Faber, Surgeon*, reissued in this series as *The Lady's Confession*, his memorable character Joseph Polwarth says, "Perhaps you are not aware that many of the seeds which fall to the ground, and do not grow, yet, strange to tell . . . retain the power of growth. . . . It is well enough known that if you dig deep in any old garden, such as this one, ancient—perhaps forgotten—flowers will appear. The fashion has changed, they have been neglected or uprooted, but all the time their life is hid below."

Indeed, through the years there were those who continued to spade the ground and upturn the soil where the long-buried seeds of George Mac-Donald's imaginative work had been concealed, each playing a unique part in bringing the forgotten novels back into public attention.

The first new shoots began to break through in earnest in the 1970's with increased reisssuings of MacDonald's works by a variety of publishers. These publications ushered in the full flowering of MacDonald's reputation for a whole new generation in the 1980's, with the republication of his adult fiction in a widespread way for the first time since his own lifetime.

As part of this resurgence of interest, it has been my privilege to edit the Classic Reprint Series of George MacDonald's novels issued since 1982 by Bethany House Publishers, in which MacDonald's original books of

400 to 600 pages—often heavily infused with old Scots dialect—have been pared down and translated, making them accessible to today's readers.

Those who have read other of his novels, or are familiar with his life through his biography, are well acquainted with MacDonald's passionate love for his Scottish homeland. Most of the novels considered by critics as his strongest achieve their excellence because they capture what must be regarded as the essential flavor of this land as viewed through MacDonald's eyes.

Certainly high in this rank must be included this book, originally published in 1881 under the title *Warlock o' Glenwarlock*, which was changed the following year to *Castle Warlock*, and is here republished as *The Laird's Inheritance*. It came at the very height of MacDonald's career, in the midst of a period of phenomenal output. *Warlock o' Glenwarlock*, one of MacDonald's longest books (714 pages), was full of Scottish brogue, and presented a memorable and vivid picture of the Highlands southwest of MacDonald's hometown of Huntly. The setting is the remote valley known as "The Cabrach," situated some twelve to fifteen miles from MacDonald's birthplace, between Rhynie and Dufftown, in what could be considered the foothills of the Grampian Mountains, the most expansive region of Scotland's central Highlands. The area is barren and solitary, beautiful only to one who loves the Highlands as MacDonald did. It made an impression on the young boy who vacationed there with his family, and he returned to it several times later in life in preparation for this book. His opening sketch of the region must stand as one of the most graphic descriptions ever to flow from his pen, and paints a true portrait of the essential mystique of the area.

There are those who voice concern about the spiritual implications of fiction, thinking that the novel is somehow less "real" than a more didactic book. The reality of fiction, however, lies on a deeper plane than mere "factness." Reality is a function of truth. And truth—however conveyed—*is* real. There is, therefore, a reality pervading the novels of George MacDonald, because the situations and characters point toward truth, and toward the One in whom is contained all truth.

By communicating his message in such a fashion, George MacDonald was following the example of his Lord. For fiction was frequently the vehicle the Lord used in order to best convey principles of life in God's kingdom. As he spoke to ordinary people, he found that telling them stories through nonfactual characters was the *best* means to express realities and truths they might not have grasped so deeply in any other way. "Do good to your neighbor" was not a teaching which originated with Jesus but had been set forth by hundreds of great men before. But it was Jesus who penetrated clearly and incisively to the very heart of the matter with his parable of the Good Samaritan, immortalizing the truth as no one before or after has ever done. In fictional format, the truth came alive for all time. Through the nonfactual, but highly *real* genre of the parable, Jesus brought spiritual principles to life.

Similarly, George MacDonald employed fiction to achieve precisely the same goal. *The Laird's Inheritance* illustrates in story form many abiding truths of the Kingdom. When the disciples asked Jesus about giving up all for him, his reply was, "No one who has left home, or land, or family for the sake of the kingdom will fail to receive many times as much in this age, and in the age to come." George MacDonald used a plot revolving around the loss of an earthly inheritance of land to tell of the deeper inheritance of God's kingdom. Whether the earthly inheritance is won or lost is beside the point; the riches of the Kingdom outshine all earthly gain. In the old castle, so insignificant in the world's eyes, good only as a ruin to him who would buy it from Cosmo's father, lies a secret—what Jesus calls "the mystery of the kingdom"—found in the heart of Cosmo's father, a secret that illuminates the riches of God's life within us. The true inheritance was there all along—but only for those with eyes to see it. The value in the eternal realm is not on the surface, but in the heart.

Yet such an inheritance is not won without sacrifice. As Jesus said, the inheritance of houses and lands and riches, in this age and in the age to come, does not come to everyone—it comes to those who have left everything for the sake of the Kingdom. Thus, the inheritance which comes to Cosmo in the end comes as a direct result of his sacrificial laying down of everything he holds dear on a worldly plane. He has to lay down his ancient family home, the land, the inheritance that in the world should rightfully be his, and lay them all on the altar. Cosmo's true and lasting inheritance comes only after he is stripped of every last vestige of self, and is ready to go out into the world as a beggar with only the shirt on his back. At that point God can step in and give him fully of Himself. For though our earthly inheritance may be lost, Jesus has said that his people will inherit the whole earth.

It is precisely the legacy of *this* inheritance—an inheritance not passed down by the hands of men, but by the hand of God into men's hearts— that Cosmo's father gives to him. Cosmo then passes it into future generations in the flow of his descendants and God's people. As has been the case since Old Testament times, the heritage of God is passed from fathers to sons, from mothers to daughters, from parents to children.

Warlock o' Glenwarlock is, like several other of MacDonald's novels, highly autobiographical. We instantly recognize in young Cosmo Warlock the thoughtful Robert Falconer, and indeed the boy George MacDonald himself. Cosmo's grandmother is reminiscent of George's own. The boy has grown up without his mother, reminding us of the death of George MacDonald's mother when he was eight. As Cosmo matures, he goes to college, turns to writing poems, and takes a job as a tutor—all of which parallels MacDonald's experience. The description of the tutorship is almost purely autobiographical, revealing almost exact insight into what we know of MacDonald's assignment in London between 1845 and 1847. And like MacDonald's, Cosmo's father managed a rather large estate of land whose fortunes were on the decline.

Most striking of all, however, is the love which exists between Cosmo and his aging father—in the heart of which pulsated the earliest attraction of the boy toward the heartbeat of God himself. Through this relationship the inheritance of God is passed, hand to hand, from father to son, just as—though Jesus performed the miracle—it was in the hands of the disciples that the loaves and fishes actually multiplied. MacDonald unquestionably draws upon the memory of his own long relationship with his father when he says: "Nobody knows what the relation of father and son may yet come to. Those who accept the relationship in Christian terms are bound to recognize that there must be in it depths more infinite than our eyes can behold, ages away from being fathomed yet. For is it not a small and finite reproduction of the loftiest mystery in human ken—that of the infinite Father and infinite Son? If man be made in the image of God, then must not human fatherhood and sonship be the earthly image of the eternal relation between God and Jesus?"

Through the mouth of Cosmo's father, the essence of what makes up the godly life is articulated. What matters, he says to his son, is not the accumulation of wealth, not the inheritance, not the land, not the castle; what matters—what comprises the life, the inheritance I give you—is to do justly, to love mercy, and to walk humbly with your God.

The desire of his father's heart is particularly moving: "But gien I've ever had onything to ca' an ambition, Cosmo, it has been that my son should be ane o' the wise, wi' faith to believe what his father had learned afore him, an' sae start farther on upo' the narrow way than his father had startit."

As reflected in Warlock's words, the Scots dialect is an intrinsic part of this book's unique Highland flavor. People often ask about the nature of the dialect, but the study of the origins of languages is a complex field, and being no linguistic historian, I can only offer some rudimentary observations. It seems there are essentially four major language groups identifiable in the Scots dialect called "doric." George MacDonald grew up with this dialect, and it found its way into at least ten of his books; MacDonald himself once referred to it as "the broad Saxon of Aberdeen." Those elements are Gaelic (an ancient Celtic language, now almost dead except for remote Highland and island regions of western Scotland and Ireland), Scandinavian, German, and English.

The Scots dialect, at first glance can be difficult to decipher, though with practice and familiarity it becomes easier. The Scots tend to drop certain consonants, and differences in pronunciation make Scots distinct from common English. Thus, "of" in a MacDonald original or a Robert Burns poem becomes *o'*, "have" becomes *hae*, "all" becomes *a'*, "so" becomes *sae*, "with" becomes *wi'*, "you" becomes *ye*, "and" becomes *an'*, "own" becomes *ain*, "young" becomes *yoong*, "how" becomes *hoo*, "about" becomes *aboot*, "well" becomes *weel*, "our" becomes *oor*, "old" becomes *auld*, and so on.

A number of words and phrases, though still English, take on a peculiarly Scottish tone or flavor when spoken—still recognizable, but altered to fit the rough, rhythmic, and rapid Scottish tongue. Thus, "where" becomes *whaur*, "from" becomes *frae*, "don't" becomes *dinna,* "can't" becomes *canna.*

Any language has colloquialisms, and Scottish has more than its share—words such as *gloamin'* (dusk), *mind* (remember), *gowk* (fool or lout), *burn* (stream), *laird* (landowner), and *bairn* (child).

And finally, many thousands of Scottish words are simply foreign to contemporary English, such as: *ken* ("know" from German), *ilk* (every), *lauchen* ("laugh" from German), *gar* (make), *lippen* (trust), *lave* (rest or remainder), *speir* (ask), *ohn* ("without" from German), *gien* (if), *gaein* ("go" or "going" from German), and *siller* (money).

Most of the dialect has been removed from the other MacDonald reprints, but in this particular book the dialect seems fundamentally linked to the Highlands and the struggle of the people who lived there in the 19th century. Thus, in *The Laird's Inheritance* most of the foreign words, phrases, and expressions have been translated, but a healthy portion of Scottish spellings of words remain, sometimes altered a bit to make them look more familiar.

Both the publisher and I encourage your response to this, and to any of George MacDonald's books. I have prepared a small pamphlet on George MacDonald, his life, and his work, which is available upon request at the address below. And for those of you interested further in the life of George MacDonald, I would point you in the direction of the Bethany House publication *George MacDonald: Scotland's Beloved Storyteller.*

God bless you!

An' noo I wiss ye a' a guid readin'!

Michael Phillips
c/o One Way Book Shop
1707 E Street
Eureka, California 95501

Dedication

Dedicated to my sons:
Robin Mark, Patrick Jeremy, and Gregory Erich.

To them I offer myself, with the prayer and hope that both their mother Judy and I might give to them in some small measure what Cosmo's father passed along to him—the exhortation to do justly, to love mercy, and to walk humbly with our God.

This inheritance I as a father would pass along to you, my sons, with all the fullness of God's blessings, in the inheritance he gives us when we lay everything on the altar for him—an inheritance not made with hands, nor an inheritance of houses, lands or possessions—but an inheritance of God's spirit dwelling within us.

And to all fathers everywhere who love their sons and daughters and desire for them the *true* inheritance of God's children as inheritors of the earth, I would also dedicate my part in this present volume.

Michael Phillips

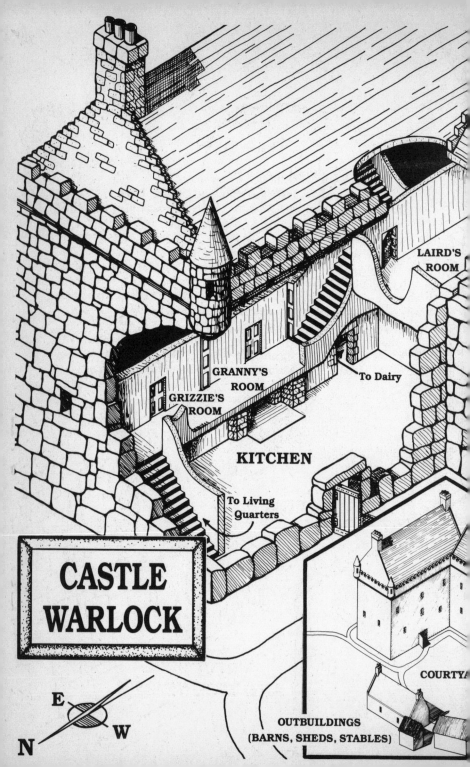

LAIRD'S
ROOM

To Dairy

GRANNY'S
ROOM

GRIZZIE'S
ROOM

KITCHEN

To Living
Quarters

CASTLE WARLOCK

COURTYA

N · E · W

OUTBUILDINGS
(BARNS, SHEDS, STABLES)

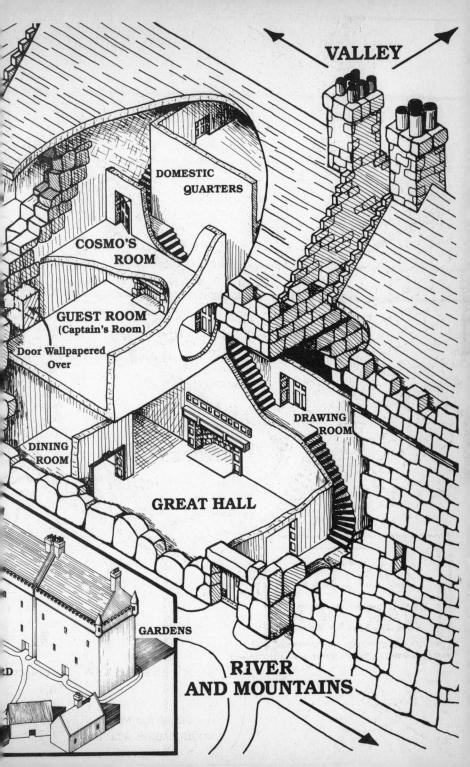

VALLEY

DOMESTIC QUARTERS

COSMO'S ROOM

GUEST ROOM
(Captain's Room)

Door Wallpapered Over

DINING ROOM

DRAWING ROOM

GREAT HALL

GARDENS

RIVER AND MOUNTAINS

1 / Castle Warlock

It was a rough, wild glen to which the family had given its name far back in times unknown, lying in the debatable land between Highlands and Lowlands. Most of its inhabitants spoke both Scots and Gaelic, and there was often to be found in them a notable mingling of the characteristics of the otherwise widely differing Celt and Teuton. The country produced more barley than wheat, more oats than barley, more heather than oats, more boulders than trees, and more snow than anything.

It was a solitary, thinly populated region on the eastern edge of the central Scottish Highlands, mostly made up of bare hills and partially cultivated glens. Each of these valleys had its own small stream, on the banks of which grew here and there a silver birch, a mountain ash, or an alder, but with nothing capable of giving much shade or shelter, except for cliffy banks and big stones. From many a spot you might look in all directions and see not a sign of habitation of either man or beast. But even then you might smell the perfume of a peat fire, although you might be long in finding out where it came from. For the houses of that region, if indeed the dwellings could be called houses, were often so hard to distinguish from the ground on which they were built that except for the smoke of fresh peats coming freely out of their wide-mouthed chimneys, it required an experienced eye to discover the human nest.

The valleys that opened northward produced little. There the snow might occasionally be seen lying on patches of still-green oats, destined now only for fodder. But where the valley ran east and west, and any tolerable ground looked to the south, there things were altogether different. There the graceful oats would wave and rustle in the ripening wind, and in the small gardens would lurk a few cherished strawberries, while potatoes and peas would be plentiful in their season.

Upon a natural terrace in such a slope to the south stood Castle Warlock.

But it turned no smiling face to the region from which came the warmth and the growth. A more grim, repellant, uninviting building would be hard to find. And yet from its extreme simplicity, its utter indifference to its own looks, its repose, its weight, and its gray historical consciousness, no one who loved old houses would have thought of calling it ugly.

The castle, like the hard-featured face of a Scottish matron, suggested no end of story and character. She might turn a defensive if not defiant face to the world, but inside where she carefully tended the fires of life, it was warm. Summer and winter the chimneys of that desolate-looking house smoked. For though the country was inclement, and the people who lived in it poor, the great sullen hills surrounding it for miles in all directions held clasped to their bare cold bosoms, exposed to all the bitterness of freezing winds and summer hail, the warmth of centuries. The peat bogs of those hills were the store closets and wine cellars of the sun, hoarding the elixir of physical life. And although the walls of the castle were so thick that in winter they kept the warmth generated within them from wandering out and being lost on the awful wastes of homeless hillside and moor, they also prevented the brief summer heat of the wayfaring sun from entering with freedom, and hence the fires were needed in the summer as well.

The house was very old, and built for more kinds of shelter than are thought of in our days. For the enemies of our ancestors were not only the cold, and the fierce wind, and the rain, and the snow, but men as well— enemies harder to keep out than the raging storm or the creeping frost. Hence, the more hospitable a house could be, the less must it look what it was: it must wear its face haughty, and turn its smiles inward.

The House of Glenwarlock, as it was sometimes called, consisted of three massive, narrow, tall blocks of building. Two of them stood end to end with but a few feet of space between, and the third stood at right angles to the two. The two which stood end to end were originally the principal parts. Hardly any windows were to be seen on the side that looked out into the valley, but in the third, of more recent construction, though it looked much the same age, there were more windows, but none in the lowest story. Narrow as these buildings were, and four stories high, they had a solid, ponderous look, suggesting such a thickness of the walls as to leave very little hollow inside for the indwellers. On the side away from the valley was a kind of court, completed by the stables and cow-houses, and toward this court were most of the windows—many of them so small that they seemed to belong more to the cottages round about the area than to a house built by the lords of the soil. The courtyard was now merely a farmyard.

At one time there must have been outer defenses to the castle, but they were no longer distinguishable to the inexperienced eye. Indeed, the win- dowless walls of the house itself seemed strong enough to repel any attack without artillery—unless the assailants got into the court. Even there, how- ever, the windows evidenced signs of having been enlarged, if not increased in number, at a later period.

In that block of the house which stood at right angles to the rest was the kitchen, whose door opened immediately onto the court. Behind the kitchen, in that part which had no windows to the valley, was the milk cellar, as they called the dairy, and places for household storage. A rough pathway ran along the foot of the walls, connecting the doors in the three different buildings. Of these, the kitchen door usually stood open. Sometimes the snow would be coming down the wide chimney, with little soft hisses in the fire, and the business of the house going on without a thought of closing it to the cold of winter, though from the open door you could not have even seen across the courtyard for the thick-falling white flakes.

At the time this narrative begins, however, summer held the old house and the older hills in its embrace. The sun poured torrents of light and heat into the valley, and the slopes of it were covered with green. The bees contented themselves with the flowers, while the heather was getting its bloom ready, and a boy of fourteen sat in a little garden. Dropped like a belt of beauty about the feet of the grim old walls, the garden lay on the south side between the house and the slope where the grain began—now with the ear half formed.

The boy sat on a big stone, which once must have had something to do with the house itself or its defenses, but which he had never known as anything except a seat for him to sit upon. His back was leaning against the old stone wall, and he was in truth meditating, although he did not look as if he were. He was already more than a budding philosopher, though he could not yet have put into recognizable shape the thought that was now passing through his mind. In brief it was this: he was thinking about how glad the bees would be when their crop of heather was ripe; then he thought how they preferred the heather to the flowers; then, that the one must taste the nicer to them than the other. This last thought awoke the question whether their taste of sweet was the same as his. If it was, he thought to himself, then there was something in the makeup of the bee that was the same with the makeup of the boy. And if that was true, then perhaps someday a boy might, if he wanted, try out the taste of being a bee for a little while.

But to look at him as he sat there, nobody would have thought he was doing anything but basking in the sun. The scents of the flowers all about his feet came and went on the eddies of the air, while the windy noises of the insects, the watery noises of the pigeons, the noises from the poultry yard, and the song of the mountain river all visited his brain as well through the portal of his ears. But at the moment the boy seemed lost in the mere fundamental satisfaction of existence.

Broad summer was indeed on the earth and the whole land was for a time bathed in sunlight. Yet although the country was his native land, and he loved it with the love of his country's poets, the consciousness of the boy could not break free from a certain strange kind of trouble—connected with, if not resulting from, the landscape before him. He was a Celt through many of his ancestors, and his mother in particular, and his soul was thus full of undefined emotion and an ever-recurring impulse to break out in song.

There were a few books in the house, among them certain of his coun-
trymen's best volumes of verse. From the reading of these had arisen this
result—that, in the midst of his enjoyment of the world around him, he
found himself every now and then sighing after a lovelier nature than that
before his eyes. In the books he read of mountains, if not wilder, yet loftier
and more savage than his own; of skies more glorious; of forests such as
he knew only from one or two old engravings in the house, upon which he
looked with a strange, inexplicable reverence. He would sometimes wake
weeping from a dream of mountains or of tossing waters.

Once with his waking eyes he saw a mist afar off, between the hills
that began the horizon. It grew rosy after the sun was down and his heart
filled as with the joy of a new discovery. Around him, it is true, the waters
rushed down from their hills, but their banks had little beauty. Not merely
did the lack of trees distress him, but the channels of the streams and rivers
near his home cut their way only through beds of rough gravel, and their
bare surroundings were desolate without grandeur—at least to eyes that
had not yet pierced to the soul of them. He had not yet learned to admire
the lucent brown of the bog waters. There seemed to be in the boy a strain
of some race used to a richer home. And yet all the time the frozen regions
of the north drew his fancy ten times more than Italy or Egypt.

His name was Cosmo, a name brought from Italy by one of the line
who had sold his sword and fought for strangers. Some of the younger
branches of the family had followed the same evil profession—chiefly from
poverty, but also in some cases from the inborn love of fighting that seems
to characterize the Celt. The last soldier of them had served the East India
Company both by sea and land: tradition more than hinted that he had
chiefly served himself. But since then the heads of the family had been
peaceful farmers of their own land, managing to draw a scanty subsistence
from an estate that had dwindled to but a twentieth of what it had been a
few centuries earlier. Even then, however, it could never have made its
proprietor rich in anything but the devotion of his tenants. Both the land
and its people were poor of body, but wealthy in what you must look beyond
the surface to find.

Growing too hot as he sat between the sun and the wall, Cosmo rose
and walked to the other side of the house beyond the courtyard, and crossing
a small patch of grass he came upon one unfailing delight in his life—a
preacher whose inarticulate voice had been at times louder in his ear than
any other since he was born. It was a mountain stream which went through
a channel of rock—almost satisfying his fastidious fancy for grandeur—
roaring, rushing, and sometimes thundering, with an arrow-like foamy
swiftness, down to the river in the glen below. The rocks were very dark
and the foam stood out brilliant against them. From the hilltop above it

came, sloping steep and far. When you looked up it seemed to come flowing from the horizon itself, and when you looked down, it seemed to have suddenly found it could no more return to the upper regions it had left high behind it, and in disgust had accepted its lot to shoot headlong into the abyss below. There was not much water in it now, but enough to make a joyous white rush through the deep-worn brown of the rock. In the autumn and spring it came down gloriously, dark and fierce, as if it sought the very center of the earth, wild with greed for an absolute rest at the end of its journey.

The boy stood and gazed into the water, as he had done hundreds of times on hundreds of days before. Whenever he grew weary he would seek this endless water, when the things about him put on their too-ordinary look. Let the hillsides around and the gravel-lined bed of the stream higher up be as dull as they might, at this particular spot it seemed inspired and sent forth by some essence of mystery and endless possibility.

There was in him an unusual combination of the power to read both the hidden internal significance of things and the scientific nature that simply obeys the laws upon it. He knew that the stream was in its second stage when it rose from the earth and rushed past the house, that it was gathered first from the great ocean, through millions of smallest ducts, up to the reservoirs of the sky, thence to descend in snows and rains, and wander down and up through the veins of the earth. But even knowing these facts, the sense of the stream's mystery had not begun to lessen in his spirit.

Happily for him, the poetic nature was not merely predominant in him, but dominant, sending itself as a pervading spirit through the scientific knowledge that otherwise would have meant little. His poetic nature illuminated the outward facts which his eyes saw with a polarized ray, revealing life's meaning at a deeper level than the physical senses could comprehend alone. All this, however, was as yet as indefinite as it was operative in him, and I am telling of him what he could not have told of himself. His poetic bent, which always sought meaning beyond facts, had not yet been turned inward upon himself.

He stood gazing, on this particular day, in a different mood than any that had come to him before. He had, as he stood, begun to see something new about this same stream. He recognized that what in the stream had drawn him from earliest childhood, with an indefinite pleasure, was the vague sense of its *mystery*—which is the form the infinite always takes first to the simplest and liveliest hearts. It was because it was *always* flowing that he loved it, because it could not stop. Where it came from was completely unknown to him, and he did not even care to know. When he later learned that it came flowing out of the dark hard earth, the mystery only grew. He imagined a wondrous cavity below in black rock, where the water gathered and gathered—nobody could think how.

And when still later he had to shift its source to the sky, it was no less marvelous, and more lovely. It was a closer binding together of the gentle earth and the awful heavens. These were a region of endless hopes and ever recurrent despairs, and that his beloved finite stream should rise there was an added joy, and gave a mighty hope with respect to the unknown. But from the sky he was sent back to the earth in further pursuit. For where did the rain come from, his books told him, but from the sea? He had read of the sea, though he had never yet seen it, and he knew it was magnificent and mighty. How was the sky fed but from the sea? How was the dark fountain fed but from the sky? How was the torrent fed but from the fountain?

As he stood thus, near the old gray walls, the nest of his family for countless generations, with the scent of the flowers in his nostrils, and the sound of the bees in his ears, it slowly began to dawn on him that he was losing something which had been a precious part of his childhood—the mysterious, infinite idea of endless, inexplicable, original birth, of out-flowing because of essential existence within! For years he had thought the stream began in the black earth—there and nowhere beyond. Now he saw that there was no original production or creation anymore. The stream was simply part of a great scientific process. There was no mystery as he had always thought. Like a great dish, the mighty ocean was skimmed of in-visible particles, which were gathered aloft into sponges, all water and no sponge. And from this, through many an airy, many an earthly channel, his ancient, self-creating fountain was fed only by what had to be, and thus it was deflowered of its mystery.

He grew very sad, and well he might. Moved by the spring eternal in himself, of which the love in his heart was but a river-shape, he turned away from the now-commonplace stream and, without knowing why, sought another of the human element about the place.

2 / The Kitchen

Cosmo entered the wide kitchen, paved with large slabs of slate. One brilliant gray-blue spot of sunlight lay on the floor, entering through a small window to the east and making the peat fire glow a deep red by contrast. Over the fire a three-legged pot hung from a great chain, with something slowly cooking in it. On the floor between the fire and sun spot lay a cat, content with fate and the world. At the corner of the fire sat an old lady in a high-backed padded chair. She had her back to the door as the boy entered, and was knitting without regarding her needles.

This was his grandmother. The daughter of a small laird in the next parish, she had started life with rather a too-large sense of her own importance by virtue of that of her family, and she had still not lived long enough to get rid of it. She had clung to it all the more since the time of her marriage because nothing had seemed to go well with the family into which she had married. She and her husband had struggled and worked hard, but to no seeming purpose; poverty had drawn its meshes closer and closer around them. They had but one son, the present laird, and when he had come of age, he succeeded to an estate yet smaller and more heavily in debt. To all appearance he would ultimately leave it to Cosmo in no better condition, if he had it to leave at all by then. From the growing fear of its final loss, he loved the place more than any of his ancestors had loved it, and his attachment to the property had descended yet stronger to his son.

But although the elder Warlock wrestled and fought against encroaching poverty, with little success, he never forgot small rights in his anxiety to be rid of large claims against him. What was possible for man to do he did to keep poverty from bearing hard on the people who were his dependents, and never master or landlord was more beloved. Such being his character and the condition of his affairs, it is not very surprising that he should have passed middle age before thinking seriously of marriage. And even then he did not fall in love in the ordinary sense of the phrase. Rather, he reasoned that it would be cowardice to fear poverty so greatly as to run the boat of the Warlocks aground, and leave the scrag end of a property and a history without a man to take them up, and possibly bear them on to redemption; for who could tell what life might be in the stock yet? Anyhow, it would be better to leave an heir to take the remnant in charge, and at least carry the name a generation further, even if it should be into yet deeper poverty. A Warlock could face his fate.

Thereupon he began to visit a woman of thirty-five, the daughter of the last clergyman of the parish, and he had been accepted by her with little hesitation. She was a brave capable woman, fully informed of the state of his affairs, and she married him in the hope of doing something to help him out of his difficulties. She had saved up a few pounds and a trifle her mother had left her, and these she placed unreservedly at his disposal. In his abounding honesty, he spent it on his creditors, bettering things for a time, and greatly relieving his mind and giving the life in him a fresh start. His marriage set the laird growing again—and that is the only final path out of oppression.

Whatever were their feelings for one another on their wedding day, those of the laird were at least those of a gentleman. But it would be a good thing indeed, if, at the end of five years, the love of most pairs who marry for love were equal to that of Warlock and his middle-aged wife. And now that she was gone, his reverence for her memory was stronger yet. Almost from the day of his marriage the miseries of life had lost half their bitterness, and had not returned even at her death.

Many outsiders, however, even those who respected him as an honest man, believed that somehow or other he must be to blame for the circumstances he was in. Either this, or God did not take care of the just man. Such was the unspoken conclusion of many who imagined that they understood the Book of Job, and who took Warlock's rare honesty to be pride or unjustifiable free-handedness instead. Hence, they came to think and speak of him as a poor creature, and soon the man, through the keen sensitivity of his nature, became aware of the fact.

He was a far finer nature than those who thus judged him, of whom some would no doubt have gotten out of their difficulties sooner than he— only he was more honorable in debt than they were out of it. His wife, a woman of strong sense with an undeveloped stratum of poetry in her heart, was able to appreciate the finer elements of his nature; and she let him see very plainly that she did. This proved a great strength and a lifting up of the head to the husband, who most of his life had been oppressed by the opposition of his mother, whom the neighbors regarded as a woman of strength and good sense. And though he now had to fight the wolf of poverty as constantly as before, things after his wife's death looked much more acceptable to him as he viewed them through the love of his wife rather than through the eyes of his neighbors.

They had been married five years before she brought him an heir to the property, and she lived five years more to train him. Then, after a short illness, she departed, and left the now aging man virtually alone with his